TRANSFORMERS
ROBOTS in DISGUISE

The Trials of Optimus Prime

by John Sazaklis & Steve Foxe

LITTLE, BROWN AND COMPANY
New York Boston

Little, Brown and Company

Hachette Book Group
1290 Avenue of the Americas, New York, NY 10104
Visit us at lb-kids.com

Little, Brown and Company is a division of Hachette Book Group, Inc.
The Little, Brown name and logo are trademarks of
Hachette Book Group, Inc.

The publisher is not responsible for websites (or their content)
that are not owned by the publisher.

First Edition: January 2016

ISBN 978-0-316-30195-4

10 9 8 7 6 5 4 3 2 1

RRD-C

Printed in the United States of America

Licensed By:

33614057656661

Sideswipe

Strongarm

Grimlock

Optimus

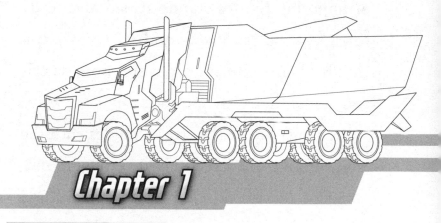

A massive red-and-blue semitruck barrels through a narrow canyon, sounding its booming horn like a rallying cry.

Three other vehicles race close behind: a boxy blue police cruiser, a sleek red sports car, and a compact yellow coupe with black stripes.

At the opposite end of the canyon, an army of imposing figures stands armed and ready to fight. The semitruck and its convoy spit clouds of dust into the air as spinning wheels tear across the sandy ground.

Moments before the truck collides with the edge of the army, its wheels leave the ground, its shape twists and changes in the air, and it reveals itself to be much more than just a vehicle—it's actually a robot in disguise!

"Autobots, attack!" the robot shouts, landing so one massive foot crushes an enemy to the ground.

The three other vehicles follow suit, lifting into the air and changing into robot modes of their own!

The army of foes reveals itself to be

composed of snarling, angular robots of a much more sinister variety: Decepticons. These terrible foes brandish wicked blades and maces.

The four Autobots stand together as a team, pushing back attackers and knocking them off one by one with energy blasters and swords. The red-and-blue leader calls the shots and looks out for his teammates.

"Bumblebee, on your left!" the leader warns, directing the yellow-and-black bot to block an incoming blow.

CRASH!

The parried Decepticon staggers back and takes out a few of its brethren as it falls.

"Sideswipe, take out that cannon!"

The nimble red bot catapults over a pile

of rocks and slices through a pair of foes readying a massive energy cannon.

THUD!

The cannon hits the canyon floor and blasts back a whole fleet of Decepticons.

CHOOM!

"Strongarm, create a perimeter for us!"

VROOM!

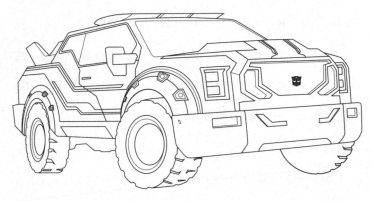

The broad-shouldered blue bot changes back into her vehicle mode and plows through the Decepticons, clearing a space for the Autobots to make a unified stand.

The enemies continue to swarm, but the four Autobots work together like one well-oiled machine.

"Good job, Autobots! But this Decepticon horde doesn't seem to be getting any smaller. We need backup."

With a flick of his wrist, the Autobot leader summons an energy shield to hold off the aggressive attackers. He speaks into the communicator embedded in his other arm.

"Fixit, we could use some extra feet on the ground right about now!"

The communicator crackles and hisses.

As if on cue, a shape darkens the sky above

the Decepticon infantry. Its shadow grows as it plummets toward the ground.

BOOOOOM!

The formidable figure smashes into the gathered Decepticons, flattening the unlucky enemies caught beneath it. The impact emits a shockwave that knocks many more off their feet.

"Thanks for dropping in, Grimlock," the leader quips.

A huge black-and-green Dinobot climbs out of the crater he just formed, grins, and joins the rumble.

"Any time!" he replies, stampeding through the horde.

The leader can't help it: He cracks a smile, too.

Even as the enemy army doubles then triples in size, he is confident that his team can stand strong against the forces of evil! He continues to bark orders and provide covering fire while countless Decepticons pour into the canyon.

Then, out of nowhere, a large swell of new enemies separates the huddled

Autobots. The leader can no longer watch his teammates' backs. He hears a pained cry ring out and then get cut short.

"Sideswipe!"

The red bot has fallen and is quickly covered by Decepticons.

Then another scream echoes through the canyon.

"Strongarm, no!" Optimus cries.

The blue police-bot drops against the canyon wall and is similarly overtaken.

The leader's resolve begins to crack, and the confidence he felt mere moments ago leaves him. He searches through the crowd for his remaining teammates. It's not too late to rally and force the Decepticons back....

A deep groan and an earthshaking thud tell him that the large Dinobot has been defeated, too.

Beating back Decepticons on every side, the leader pushes through to the yellow-and-black bot's position. Blades slice and maces smash against his plating as he prioritizes the search for his last standing teammate over his own safety.

Cannons fire around him into the canyon walls, throwing dust and rock shards into the air. Optimus hears a familiar cry and sees a blur of yellow fall toward the ground.

"Bumblebee!" the leader shouts. With a wide swoop of his sword, he knocks back a swarm of enemies to reveal the crumpled shape of the last remaining member of his team.

"No, not you, too," he whispers, kneeling beside his friend. The yellow-and-black bot barely moves.

"Optimus..." Bumblebee struggles to speak.

The leader looks down at his injured comrade.

"Optimus, the others..."

The dazed Decepticons pick themselves up and surround the duo. Escape is impossible.

The Autobot leader, Optimus, is soon covered on all sides, stumbling under the combined weight of his faceless assailants.

He struggles and strains to hear what Bumblebee has to tell him over the din of the Decepticon army.

And suddenly, the message is clear:

"Optimus... you failed us!"

Chapter 2

For a few nanocycles, everything is dark.
Then, one by one, the Decepticons piled on top of Optimus blink out of existence, like the static hum of a television set when it is unplugged.

The defeated Autobots are the only ones left in the canyon.

Optimus eyes the broken frames of his teammates, until those, too, fade away.

The leader looks down into his arms just in time to catch the last hazy shadow of Bumblebee before he disappears from sight.

"Not as ready as you thought you were, eh, hotshot?"

A voice rings out from the canyon walls above.

The next time it speaks, it comes from a different direction. "Hate to be so hard on you, but taking it easy never helped anyone."

Optimus squints up into the harsh light, searching for the source of the voice.

"Down here, big guy," the voice says, suddenly appearing behind the Autobot.

The voice's owner is a short green bot with bulky shoulders and a wide, square jaw. He hovers cross-legged a few feet off the canyon floor.

As he speaks, the canyon walls start to dissolve in a flurry of light, until the space around the two bots becomes a vast, nondescript void.

"My teammates…" the leader mumbles, as if waking up from a dream.

"Not your *real* teammates, Optimus, just holograms of bots you barely know," the floating figure replies. "Except for that yellow one, I guess. And *maybe* I went too far by giving it dialogue processors."

Optimus narrows his optics.

"Those bots are Bumblebee's teammates. That makes them my allies. And I couldn't save them."

The green bot chuckles.

"Well, they're still holograms. Just like all the Decepticons who whooped your rear bumper. Not that it makes your new dents and scratches feel any better, I'm sure."

Optimus surveys the damage he accumulated during the simulated battle.

Despite the seemingly sharp weapons of the holographic Decepticons, his wounds are no more than surface-deep. The simulation wasn't meant to actually harm Optimus, only to test him.

The other bot waves his hand and a

shimmering light passes over Optimus, fixing any signs of damage.

"Thank you, Micronus," Optimus says, slightly bowing his head in respect. "The Realm of the Primes is still so disorienting to me. I know I am here to train and prepare myself for the battle ahead, but these simulations feel so real...."

"Would they do you any good if they didn't?" Micronus shoots back.

Micronus is one of the Thirteen, the

original Transformers created by Primus to battle Unicron eons ago. Each was designated a Prime and given unique powers and abilities.

Micronus is the very first Mini-Con, a race of small Cybertronians imbued with the ability to enhance the powers of their allies.

Ever since Optimus Prime made the ultimate sacrifice to restore the AllSpark to their home planet of Cybertron, he has existed in the Realm of the Primes. Here, he strengthens himself physically and mentally for an ominous and unknown battle to come. Micronus has served as his mentor...and he hasn't gone easy on his pupil.

"Now shake it off. We're far from done here," Micronus says.

"I need to return to Earth," Optimus replies. "Every day that passes is another day that the Decepticons could strike. Bumblebee and the others need me."

Micronus scrutinizes his student.

"Do they need you, or do you need *them*?"

Optimus doesn't respond.

"Pellechrome wasn't built in a millennium,"

Micronus says. "And you just royally scrapped that training sequence. I'm not exactly shooting confidence in your abilities out of my tailpipe right now."

"I understand your reservations, Micronus," Optimus replies. "But I've faced Megatron. I've stood against Unicron. And now it's time for me to rejoin my team on Earth."

"You're serious, aren't you?" Micronus asks with a scoff. "All right, I'll convene with the other Primes to discuss this. No promises, though. You're still rough around the grill as far as I'm concerned."

Before Optimus can thank the elder bot, Micronus fades away in a glimmer of sparks, leaving Optimus alone in the Realm of the Primes.

An unknown distance away, Micronus reappears, hovering in the shadow of a council of immense bots: the Primes. Of these powerful beings, only Micronus has chosen to reveal himself to Optimus.

"Okay, fellas," Micronus says, comfortable among his brethren. "The kid is getting antsy. He wants to return to Earth."

A booming laugh breaks out among the shadowed Primes.

"He's bold enough to suggest that he is ready after failing against a mob of your conjured Decepticons?" a deep voice asks.

"'Bold' or 'stupid'?" a cackling voice chimes in.

Micronus turns toward its source.

"Optimus is far from stupid, Liege Maximo," he retorts. "He is one of our best chances at beating back the growing darkness. Not that I would expect *you* to care."

The figure with the deep voice speaks again to Micronus.

"You are right to believe in Optimus's potential, but he is not yet ready. We have been too easy on him, and his progress has faltered as a result. We charge you, Micronus, with making his training more rigorous. When he does return to Earth, he must be *prepared*."

"Your wish is my command sequence,

brothers," Micronus replies, fading away to give Optimus the disappointing news.

As the other Primes drift off, Liege Maximo remains. He pulls his cape around his frame and flexes the imposing hornlike appendages on his head.

"Perhaps I *should* care about Optimus's training...." Liege Maximo says aloud to himself, forming a plan. "After all, having a new plaything to manipulate might help relieve my boredom!"

Chapter 3

"Well, don't act surprised," Micronus tells
Optimus as the Autobot leader processes his
disappointment. "We didn't bring you here
for scraps and giggles, we brought you here to
prepare to face unimaginable evil."

"Worse than Unicron and Megatron?"

Optimus asks. "Because I defeated them—*with* my team. I trust Bumblebee to protect Earth in my absence, but what if this great evil strikes before the Primes think I'm ready?"

Micronus hovers high above Optimus. He waves his hands and four large bots rise out of the ground. Each is outfitted with hefty shoulder cannons.

"You think you're ready? Prove it."

Optimus flexes his pistons.

"Bring on the slag-heaps!" he shouts.

"Oh, we're going to make things a little more interesting now," Micronus responds.

He lets out a laugh and waves his hand.

Glimmering buildings rise out of the ground, creating an approximation of a metropolis on Earth. With another wave of his hand, smaller holograms of humans appear.

"Think you can keep these little ones safe?" As soon as Micronus issues his challenge, the four weaponized bots split up and dart after different groups of the holographic civilians.

Optimus springs into action!

He chases after the biggest bot and leaps onto its back. Optimus unsheathes his energy sword and wedges it under the bot's shoulder cannon.

SHTICK!

The bot tries to shake Optimus loose, but Optimus uses all of his weight to pry the cannon loose from its shoulder mount.

With a backward leap, Optimus lands

with the cannon in one arm and holsters his sword.

Optimus tugs on the cannon's firing mechanism, blasting the big bot off its feet in a noisy explosion of energy.

CHOOM!

"One down, three to go!"

With one group of civilians safe, Optimus hoists the cannon onto his shoulder and aims it toward another adversary.

BOOM!

Optimus drops the cannon and darts after the remaining robots.

"Don't get cocky, Optimus!" Micronus shouts.

"Oh no, please *do* get cocky, Autobot," another voice whispers just out of audio receptor distance. "And reckless. It will be much more fun if you're reckless!"

Unbeknownst to Micronus and Optimus, they've got an unseen guest watching them: Liege Maximo!

Liege Maximo is not necessarily evil, but his petty jealousy and boredom motivate him to be a tricky troublemaker.

While Optimus chases down the third bot, Liege Maximo pulls the fourth one into an alley. He twitches his horns and reprograms the bot to be much more vicious in its attacks! He also installs a few surprises for Optimus.

His meddling accomplished, Liege Maximo slips away out of sight. He settles into a spot high up on one of the fake buildings where he can watch the chaos unfold unobserved.

Just then, Optimus subdues the third bot, saving the humans from being harmed.

"Last one! It's closing time!"

The brave Autobot leader dashes through the holographic streets, eager to find his final foe.

Before he can, a cannon blast knocks him off his feet and sends him flying into a nearby wall.

CRASH!

"Ouch! These simulations aren't playing around!"

Optimus climbs to his feet and rushes toward the source of the blast.

When the bot charges up for a second cannon blast, Optimus summons his energy shield.

The bot fires, but Optimus deflects the blast.

FWOOM!

The Autobot leader draws his sword and watches his attacker's arms suddenly turn into spinning saw blades!

"Saving the worst for last, Micronus?" Optimus asks under his breath.

Micronus is puzzled by this development.

"I may be many eons old," he says to himself, "but I'm pretty sure I didn't summon attack-bots with saw-blade arms...."

Meanwhile, Optimus pedals backward, stepping out of the path of the spinning blades.

The attack-bot presses forward, preparing to fire its cannon again!

Optimus pulls up his shield, just as a large

volley of energy—much larger than before— shoots directly at Optimus.

His shield splinters, but not before reflecting the bulk of the blast, aiming it back at the bad bot.

KABOOM!

When the dust clears, Optimus finds himself in the wreckage of one of the holographic buildings. He stumbles into the street and sees what's left of his opponent: a lone saw blade rolling across the pavement.

Optimus didn't survive unscathed, though. His injuries feel much more serious than before, as if this simulation was actually meant to hurt him!

Luckily, none of the simulated humans were in this part of the city. Despite the damage he sustained, Optimus feels good about his training session.

"Looking sharp, Optimus," Micronus says, hovering down to the Autobot's level. "Did you find this session...particularly challenging?"

Optimus doesn't want to admit to his mentor that he's actually hurt. If the Primes don't think he's mastering their tasks, they won't let him return to Earth. The Autobot leader grimaces through the pain.

"It was a pretty close shave, but nothing I couldn't handle."

Micronus is suspicious—not of his pupil's abilities, but of the attack drone's weapons.

Still, the drill is complete. He waves his hands and the cityscape and its humanlike inhabitants fade away. A second gesture heals some of the dents and scrapes on Optimus's frame, but the deeper wounds inflicted by the fourth bot still ache.

As the last of the buildings fade away, Micronus thinks he spots something in one of the higher windows.

But as quickly as he notices it, it's gone.

A trick of the light, he thinks.

A moment later, some distance away within the expansive Realm of the Primes, Liege Maximo reappears. The wicked Prime laughs uncontrollably, pleased with himself for manipulating Micronus's training exercise with Optimus—and getting away with it.

He summons a crude mock version of the

Autobot leader. He throws his cape over his shoulder and begins to slowly pace away from the motionless mannequin.

"Optimus, Optimus, Optimus...so eager to prove yourself that you'll suffer through pain," Liege Maximo says aloud.

As he paces, he pulls a small handful of dangerously sharp darts out of a holster near his waist. "I suppose the one question left to answer..."

Liege Maximo spins on his heels and lets the darts fly. They embed themselves in the fake Optimus's head!

"...is just how much pain can you take?"

Chapter 4

Micronus leads Optimus through the Realm of the Primes. Although he doesn't mention it, Micronus notices that the Autobot leader is walking with a slight limp.

"It's not time for you to return to Earth, Optimus," Micronus says. "But that doesn't mean you can't check in on things."

Micronus stops at the base of a hill. He waves his hands in a familiar gesture and then urges Optimus to climb the hill. The Autobot leader does as instructed and finds a reflecting pool at the top. Through it, he can see Earth!

"I wouldn't count sheepbots for too long, but I think you earned a break," Micronus says, turning to give Optimus some privacy. "Consider it a reminder of whom you're fighting for."

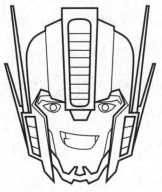

The Prime disappears, leaving Optimus alone with the portal.

As Optimus peers into it, his friends begin to come into view....

"Go long, Sideswipe!" Rusty Clay shouts, running backward and winding his arm up to throw a football.

"Let it rip, Rusty!" Sideswipe hollers, nimbly running through the junk-filled aisles of the scrapyard.

Rusty is the young son of Denny Clay, owner of the scrapyard that Bumblebee and his team of Autobots call home while on Earth.

Sideswipe was a bit of a troublemaker

back on Cybertron, but even though he has a bit of an authority problem, he's an invaluable member of the team.

Rusty lets the ball fly through the air. It tears through the sky in a perfect arc...until a pair of giant metal jaws chomp down on it, instantly deflating it!

"HOLE IN ONE!" Grimlock shouts, the now-useless rubber of the ball dangling from his open mouth.

Grimlock is a reformed Decepticon. What he lacks in common sense, he makes up for in strength, loyalty, and enthusiasm.

"Yeah, hole in one, all right—hole in the one lob-ball we had!" Sideswipe says, yanking the remains from Grimlock's teeth.

"That was a football, not a lob-ball, Sideswipe," Rusty says with a frown. "And 'hole in one' is from a different sport...."

"Don't feel bad, Russell Clay," Fixit says, patting Rusty on the back. "I can fit...flip... fix it right up!"

Sideswipe hands the deflated ball to Fixit, the team's Mini-Con.

Fixit was the pilot of the *Alchemor* maximum-security prison transport ship that crashed on Earth, releasing Decepticon prisoners across the planet. The crash also damaged Fixit's speech modules, which is why he sometimes trims…tricks…trips over words!

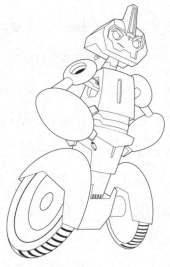

"That's okay, Fixit. I'm sure my dad has some 'vintage' footballs around here somewhere," Rusty says.

"Nonsense! I'll repair this in two nano-cycles."

Fixit shifts his hand into a complex drill tool.

Before Rusty can stop him, Fixit has somehow mangled the ball even worse.

"Oh my! This doesn't seem to have worked at all!"

Across the scrapyard, Bumblebee sits at the command center computers with Strongarm, his eager, law-abiding second-in-command. While the others play, Bumblebee and Strongarm use the computer's sensors to search for Decepticon fugitives roaming the area.

"Strongarm, why don't you go join the other bots?" Bumblebee suggests to his lieutenant. "It looks like our Decepticon pals are lying low today. You should relax a little."

"No, thank you, sir," Strongarm replies, straightening into a salute. "My place is at your side."

"I think you should take your place a little less seriously once in a while, cadet."

Strongarm frowns.

"How about this: I order you to go keep an eye on the others," Bumblebee says, approaching the request from a different angle. "And if you happen to have fun in the course of your mission, that's permissible."

Strongarm maintains a serious look on her face.

"Sir, yes, sir!"

Bumblebee shakes his head as the cadet exits the command center.

"Was I ever that eager with Optimus?" Bumblebee wonders aloud to himself.

Back in the Realm of the Primes, Optimus

smiles down at his former lieutenant.

"You certainly were, Bumblebee."

"Why aren't you ever that excited to see me?" Micronus asks, suddenly appearing in front of Optimus. Micronus gestures at the portal and it begins to close, cutting off Optimus's brief glance at his Autobot teammates on Earth.

"Bumblebee has assembled a good team

down there," Optimus says. "I don't know if he realizes it yet, but he has."

"I'm glad someone is adequately filling your stabilizers while you're away," Micronus says. "But it's time for you to reassemble and get some rest. I have new trials planned for you once you've recharged."

As Optimus limps away from the hill, following the hovering form of Micronus, a third figure slinks up to where the portal just closed.

"You're going to be even more fun than I had hoped, Optimus!" Liege Maximo whispers, horns twitching.

He waits for the two bots to clear the area and then repeats the gesture that Micronus made. Immediately, the portal reopens, focusing back on Bumblebee sitting at the computer console.

"It's showtime!"

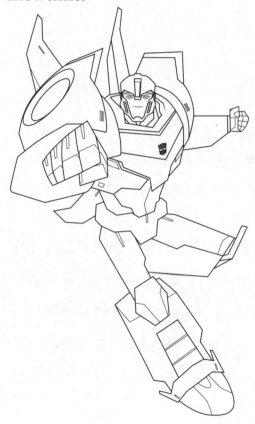

Chapter 5

Bumblebee taps at the keys, his optics growing weary from staring at facts and figures spread across multiple screens.

The other Autobots, now joined by Strongarm, are messing around elsewhere in the scrapyard.

The mysterious and stoic Autobot Drift, a

recent ally, is off on his own scouting mission with his two Mini-Cons, Slipstream and Jetstorm.

Denny Clay is in the diner he calls home, cataloging barbarian toys from the eighties that he purchased online.

Unbeknownst to Bumblebee, the scheming Liege Maximo is looking down on him from the Realm of the Primes, outside of normal space and time.

Liege Maximo delights in causing disruption, and he knows now that Bumblebee and Optimus hold a deep bond of respect for each other.

Summoning his powers of manipulation, Liege Maximo creates an image of Optimus on one of Bumblebee's screens. Bumblebee is so used to processing data that he doesn't think much of it.

"When did I pull up this profile of Optimus?" Bumblebee asks out loud to himself.

He attempts to click it away, but he can't find a way to dismiss the file. As his confusion mounts, a familiar voice echoes through the speakers.

"BUMBLEBEE!"

Bumblebee nearly topples backward!

Since Optimus awoke in the Realm of the Primes, he has occasionally appeared to Bumblebee to deliver messages of encouragement or warnings against danger. But showing up in Bumblebee's computer is a first!

"Optimus? You startled me!" Bumblebee says, calming down. "What's the glitch? Do we need to prepare for an attack?"

"YES, BUMBLEBEE!" the voice booms once more.

Bumblebee is nervous—this isn't like the previous visions he's received.

"YOU MUST PREPARE FOR A TERRIBLE ATTACK!"

The yellow Autobot shouts into his wrist

communicator for his team to assemble in the command center immediately. He turns back to the screen.

"What kind of attack, Optimus? From whom?"

"FROM ME!"

The image of Optimus begins to laugh terribly before turning to static. The speakers fuzz and shoot sparks across the floor.

Bumblebee is stunned silent.

Before he can process what just happened, the rest of his team pours into the command center.

"What's wrong, sir?" Strongarm asks, the first to Bumblebee's side.

"I...I saw..." Bumblebee can't think of a way to explain what he just witnessed.

When he first started seeing Optimus, his teammates weren't sure if they believed him or not. It wasn't until the Autobot leader appeared in full metal form to help them out that everyone accepted it.

There's no way they're going to believe Optimus just showed up to warn Bumblebee of an attack—from Optimus himself!

"What did you see, Bee?" Sideswipe asks, impatient to know what's going on.

"I saw..."

"Skinkbomb!" Fixit shouts, pointing at the

screen behind Bumblebee. "Our leader must have spotted Skinkbomb, the Decepticon demolitions expert. His radar blip just appeared on-screen!"

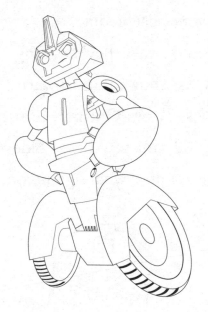

Fixit's treads roll across the floor to the console. His digits tip-tap across the keys and pull up a profile for Skinkbomb. The

Decepticon is broad and stocky, with reptilian features and a wide, squat tail.

Fixit chuckles to himself.

"No wonder Bumblebee is speechless—Skinkbomb has quite an ugly mug!"

"You got that right," Grimlock says. "And that tail don't look too pretty neither."

"Skinkbomb was apprehended for unauthorized demolitions on Cybertron," Fixit informs the group. "But he's explosive even without his bombs. His tail is actually a miniature warhead of its own, which he can detach at will and regrow by consuming metal and oil."

Strongarm looks expectantly at Bumblebee, who is still rattled by the sinister message from Optimus.

"Um, sir..." Strongarm says, nudging Bumblebee discreetly.

The Autobot leader realizes his team is staring at him.

"Oh, right," he mumbles. "Let's, um, get out there and...arrest...this Decepticon."

The other bots exchange puzzled looks. Their leader's lame attempt at trying to coin a catchphrase just now was especially pathetic.

"Wow," Sideswipe whispers to Grimlock. "Bee really dropped the lob-ball on that one, didn't he?"

Moments later, the Autobots are rolling out of the scrapyard.

According to Fixit's monitoring devices, Skinkbomb is at the base of the Crown City Bridge. Bumblebee and his team need to move fast to prevent catastrophe!

When they arrive, Strongarm, along with Denny and Rusty in police uniform disguises, head for the bridge's entrance to block oncoming traffic and clear the road of civilians.

Bumblebee leads Sideswipe and Grimlock under the bridge to confront Skinkbomb along the water's edge.

Strongarm, in police cruiser vehicle mode, uses her megaphone to help sell the urgency of the evacuation above. Within a few minutes, the bridge is cleared.

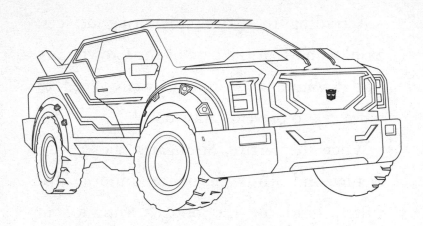

Rusty and Denny stay topside to maintain the barriers while Strongarm heads to the base of the bridge to join her teammates in a volatile battle.

KABOOM!

Skinkbomb is slow and bulky, but he is handy with explosives. Each time the Autobots gets close, Skinkbomb hurls a small grenade to keep them at a distance.

"Boom! You get an explosive! You get an explosive!" Skinkbomb vibrates with a deep, unhinged laugh. "I'll blow us all to bolts before I go back to lockup!"

Skinkbomb chucks a bomb toward Bumblebee, who dives out of the way in time to miss most of the blast.

The Autobot lands in the water below the

bridge. As he lifts himself out of the murk, a face slowly comes into focus through the rippling water.

"BUMBLEBEE!"

Bumblebee rubs his optics, convinced that it must be a trick of the water.

"I'VE SEEN THE ERROR OF MY WAYS, BUMBLEBEE," the vision of Optimus says to his former protégé. "ALIGNING OURSELVES WITH THE WEAK AUTOBOTS WAS A MISTAKE."

Bumblebee looks back at his team.

Grimlock, Sideswipe, and Strongarm are working together to get close enough to apprehend Skinkbomb, but the Decepticon is holding them off.

"What are you talking about Optimus? You're a hero!"

"I WAS A FOOL!" the voice bellows. "BUT NOW I AM STRONG."

Optimus's optics take on an eerie glow.

Bumblebee glances at his team once more as they struggle against their powerful foe. In battle against a dangerous Decepticon like Skinkbomb, every nanocycle counts!

He wants to go help them, but he's frozen in anticipation of what this vision of Optimus will say next.

"NOW…I AM A DECEPTICON!"

Chapter 6

The Autobot leader is distracted by his
vision of an evil Optimus.

"Watch out, Bee!" Sideswipe warns.

The agile young bot tackles Bumblebee,
pushing him out of the way of one of Skinkbomb's explosives.

BOOM!

Bumblebee gets slammed into a bridge support pillar by the force of the blast. His audio receptors are ringing and his entire chassis is rattling. He is dinged up but otherwise unharmed.

But what about his teammate?

"Sideswipe!"

Bumblebee splashes through the shallow water to Sideswipe's side. The ninja-like Autobot is badly injured—having taken the brunt of the explosion while saving Bumblebee.

"Sideswipe, I need to get you out of here."

The battered bot struggles to speak.

"Don't sweat it, Bee…just take out…that Decepti…" Sideswipe's voice trails off.

Bumblebee props Sideswipe against a bridge support pillar and rushes back to the fight.

Grimlock and Strongarm are still dodging explosive blasts, seeking any opportunity to dash in and attack Skinkbomb.

When the dangerous Decepticon spots

a very angry and determined Bumblebee charging in his direction, he knows his luck is running out.

"Uh-oh, looks like it's time to bring the house down!"

The demolitions expert spins around and reveals that his bulbous tail is lighting up— the explosives within it are armed!

With a grinding of gears, the tail comes loose from Skinkbomb's frame.

"Hasta la vista, babies!" Skinkbomb shouts as he makes a break for it. "Exit, stage left!"

Bumblebee grinds to a halt a few feet from the tail.

Grimlock and Strongarm race after Skinkbomb, but their leader instructs them otherwise.

"There's no time, Autobots! Find cover, now!"

The flashing lights on the detached tail accelerate.

Team Bee runs toward the support pillars,

with its leader carrying Sideswipe over his shoulders.

The four Autobots duck behind the thick concrete just as—

BOOOOOOOOOM!

The force of the blast makes the bridge groan and sway.

Luckily, Strongarm and Grimlock were able to lead Skinkbomb far enough away that there is no structural damage.

Unfortunately, the explosion gave the Decepticon plenty of time to escape.

With an injured Autobot and no arrest, the mission is officially a failure.

The bots shift back into vehicle mode (and Grimlock into Dino mode), pick up the

Clays, and return to the scrapyard with their wounded comrade.

In the Realm of the Primes, Liege Maximo

cackles with delight. By briefly pretending to be Optimus, he has sown discord among the Autobots on Earth.

"They must think their fearless leader has brain rust!"

Pleased with himself, Liege Maximo closes the portal to Earth and travels through the Realm to check in on the *real* Optimus and his training under Micronus.

He finds the pair meditating atop two towering pillars.

"This doesn't look challenging *at all*," Liege Maximo whispers.

He uses his immense abilities to create a small fleet of sharp-limbed drone robots. Using their bladed arms, they quickly scurry up the pillars.

Without warning, the drones attack Optimus!

Before the Autobot can react, several of their blades slice against his frame, leaving painful rivets in the steel.

SLASH! SLASH!

"Micronus! Are you warning me never to let my guard down?"

Optimus summons his shield and unsheathes his sword.

The drones continue to leap at him with

thrashing claws. He blocks incoming blows and attacks back when he can, careful to maintain his balance atop the massive column.

Micronus is jarred out of his meditation by the clashing of blades. He looks across the divide between their pillars to find Optimus embroiled in battle against a small army of bladed assailants—bots he did not summon himself.

The pint-sized Prime rises from his position on the pillar. With one wave of his hand, he lifts Optimus up into the air. With another, he removes both pillars, sending the sharp little attackers plummeting. They smack into the ground, shatter into flecks of light, and disappear.

SKEESH!

Micronus lowers himself down and brings Optimus with him.

"I don't understand," Optimus says. "Did I perform the trial wrong?"

"No, Optimus," Micronus responds. "You weren't wrong—the attackers were. I didn't create those bots. Which means something is rotten in the Realm. Someone is interfering with your training."

Optimus looks around him for a likely

culprit, but the Realm of the Primes is an immense, shadowy place with an ever-changing landscape. Anyone wishing to hide would have plenty of places to do so.

"I need to convene with the rest of the Primes and discuss this troubling development."

Micronus creates a large, flat-topped pyramid out of the ground.

"You stay here. I don't want you caught by surprise until we find out who's behind this."

Optimus climbs to the top of the pyramid, where he can see most of the land around him.

"Micronus, are the other Primes testing me, too? I…I don't want to fail them."

"If they were, I'd know," Micronus replies.

"And wrecking you here wouldn't do us any good back on Earth or Cybertron."

Micronus points to Optimus's very real dents and scratches when he says this.

The Prime disappears, leaving Optimus alone.

Far in the distance, Liege Maximo grins wickedly, excited that his new plaything is all his for the moment!

Back on Earth, Strongarm and Grimlock

help Bumblebee load Sideswipe onto Fixit's repair table. The brash young Autobot is badly banged up and is drifting in and out of rest mode.

"I've got him from here, Bee," the Mini-Con

says cheerfully. "Nothing some elbow grease can't fix! And some Energon infusions. And an extensive diagnostic repair kit—"

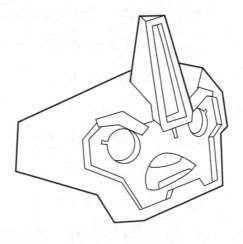

"We get it, Fixit," Bumblebee interrupts. "Just make sure he's okay, all right? It's my fault he's injured. I was distracted and Sideswipe saved me from getting hurt by taking the blast himself."

Grimlock and Strongarm look away.

They're not used to their leader expressing this kind of regret.

"I want you two to stay by his side," Bumblebee tells them. "I'm going to track down Skinkbomb's whereabouts so we can put that dangerous dynamite stick back on ice." The Autobot leader takes another look at Sideswipe and walks out of the repair center.

"Grimlock, did you see what distracted Bee during the fight?" Strongarm asks.

"Uhh…it kind of looked like he was staring at his own reflection," Grimlock replies. "I like to look at my handsome face, too, but there's a time and a place, ya know?"

Fixit eavesdrops on Strongarm and Grimlock's conversation while he works away at repairing Sideswipe.

"Was Bumblebee acting dazed and confused without rear…fear…I mean, clear reason?" he asks.

Strongarm and Grimlock consider for a second, then respond in unison, "Yes."

"Have there been moments recently when

Bee seemed to be distant and aloof, as if he were in his own world?"

Strongarm and Grimlock think about it again, remembering Bee's odd behavior in the command center before the mission. They reply in the affirmative again.

"Ah, it's very simple, then," Fixit says. "Our leader must be suffering from brain rust!"

Chapter 7

Strongarm and the other members of Bumblebee's beleaguered team on Earth aren't the only bots grappling with concern for one of their own.

Back in the Realm of the Primes, Micronus again consults with his brothers about Optimus's training.

"You told me to take it harder on the kid, not turn him into spare parts," Micronus says, hovering in front of the shadowy figures of the Primes. "And if you entrust me to train him, you should let me know if you're going to stick your sprockets into the proceedings."

Micronus can't help a note of wounded pride from entering his voice.

"Has there been…an incident?" a deep voice asks.

Micronus looks at the Primes with mounting confusion.

"You mean to tell me you haven't been sending your own bots after Optimus?" the miniscule bot asks. "Real aggressive ones, loaded up with pointy blades?"

The gathered Primes look at one another for answers, but none claims responsibility.

"Wait a minute," Micronus says. "Where is he? Where is that no-good, horn-headed, backstabbing son of a slag-heap?"

The Primes step out of the shadows, revealing one fewer figure than the last time Micronus met with them.

"Where is Liege Maximo?"

Back at the pyramid, Optimus takes advantage of his solitude to practice sword techniques. Time does not pass the same in the Realm of the Primes as it does on Earth or Cybertron, and the Autobot leader finds that he rarely needs to rest.

Optimus's desire for justice and peace has always been enough to drive him, but he misses working alongside his teammates.

Unfortunately, Liege Maximo has figured this out from watching Optimus check in on Bumblebee and the crew on Earth, and he hatches a diabolical idea.

With a stir of his horns and a wave of his

hands, the manipulative mischief-maker conjures up an approximation of Bumblebee, visually identical to the Autobot stationed back on Earth, except with a pair of creepy red optics.

Liege Maximo imbues the false bot with a devilish mean streak and directs it toward Optimus's pyramid!

His plan in motion and a smirk on his face, Liege Maximo gathers his cape and retreats to a safe viewing distance. He creates a curtain of fog to hide his presence.

"And now it's time for the second act!" he says.

In between thrusts of his blade, Optimus picks up on a slight noise, like treads scraping against the mysterious bedrock of the Realm. The red-and-blue hero glances around, noticing the gathered fog for the first time.

"You're not going to catch me off guard, Micronus!" Optimus shouts into the near-total silence. He swings around with his blade drawn…and comes face-to-face with Liege Maximo's cruel creation!

"Bumblebee?!"

Optimus is shocked at first, but remembers

Micronus's holograms of his teammates during the canyon simulation.

The Autobot leader is a fast learner and a quick thinker. A trick like this can't fool him for long!

"Did Micronus create you to test my emotions?" Optimus asks.

The fake Bumblebee rushes forward and grabs Optimus by the shoulders.

"I'm real, Optimus!" Bumblebee says. "And I'm here because we failed! Earth is lost!"

The Autobot leader staggers back out of the fake Bumblebee's grasp. His confidence that this isn't the Bumblebee he knows is slightly shaken.

"We couldn't stop what was coming without your help. Now the others are gone, and

I'm stuck here in this weird place with you," the false friend explains.

Optimus hesitates, but stands firm that the feeling in his bolts is true.

"I don't believe you," he says. "Tell me something that only Bumblebee would know, something that will prove to me that you're the bot I've trusted by my side in the past— and that what you're saying about Earth is true."

The imposter bot stares at Optimus.

Some distance away, Liege Maximo fumes with fury.

"Scrap! Curse that Optimus and his resistance to my trickery. I'll just have to use a little force!"

The Prime upgrades his creation to unnerve Optimus even more.

"Come on, buddy, you *know* it's me, deep in your spark," Bumblebee says, shaking the bigger bot's frame. "It's me...your ol' pal BEE!"

The evil imposter leaps at Optimus, red optics glaring.

With the back of his sword, Optimus clocks the phony Bumblebee in the noggin.

BONK!

"Is that how you treat an old friend?" the dazed doppelgänger whines.

Optimus unleashes a powerful roundhouse kick that sends Bumblebee tumbling off the pyramid. He slides down the side like a skater grinding a pipe, shooting up sparks as he goes.

By the time he reaches the bottom, the mock Bumblebee has faded away like the other constructs of the Realm.

The fog recedes and disappears, too.

"Micronus!" Optimus yells. "Micronus, what sort of test is this?"

"No test of mine, for Solus Prime's sake," Micronus says, suddenly appearing behind Optimus.

With an aggressive wave of his hand, the pyramid rapidly flattens.

"Optimus, we have a big problem, and his name is Liege Maximo."

Some distance away from Optimus and

Micronus, Liege Maximo continues to seethe.

"That humorless, rust-headed reject is ruining everything!" Liege Maximo says aloud to himself. "This realm is *endlessly* boring and the other Primes are no fun at all. Now the first new plaything to come along in eons is already growing wise to my tricks!"

The horned bot paces back and forth, considering his options.

In the midst of his stomping, Liege Maximo notices that he is near a small hill. He climbs the gentle slope and stares down into the pool at the top of it, the perfect plan leaping instantly into his manipulative mind.

"If Optimus won't play along, I'll turn my attention back to these other new toys."

With a wicked wave of his hand, the pool at Liege Maximo's feet stirs and reveals a window to another place, far away from the Realm of the Primes: the scrapyard on Earth, with the real Bumblebee and the other bots!

Chapter 8

Bumblebee enters the command center cautiously, remembering his vision of an unhinged Optimus. He doesn't want to believe that these garish glimpses of his former leader are real, but they certainly felt like they were....

Even if the visions were just hallucinations

brought on by stress and pressure, they threw Bumblebee off his game during the Autobots' battle with Skinkbomb. He takes full responsibility for the injuries Sideswipe sustained, and the only way to make it up to him is to track down the escaped Decepticon!

Bumblebee runs his digits over the keys of the computer console, bringing it to electronic life. He pulls up Fixit's tracking software and sets the radius as wide as it will go.

The outskirts of Crown City, where the team first fought Skinkbomb, are clear of Decepticon life-forms. The forest around the scrapyard is likewise deserted.

The quarry on the other side of the forest, however, shows one big red blip on the radar!

"Bingo!" Bumblebee shouts. "I'm taking you down personally, you overgrown lizard-bot!"

As Bumblebee moves to gather the rest of his team, the red blip on the radar flickers in and out like a dying lightbulb.

The Autobot leans in closer to examine the screen. The light flickers again, and then a second red light pops into existence a short distance from the first.

"A second Decepticon!" Bumblebee says. "Skinkbomb must have an ally!"

The two lights flicker and blink in unison like a pair of eyes.

"Are they trying to disguise their signals? I've got to get the others and track these two down before they disappear!"

Just then, a loud, familiar voice pipes through the speakers.

"WHY DO YOU FIGHT AGAINST US, BUMBLEBEE?" the voice asks.

Bumblebee recoils from the screen.

An outline appears around the two red lights, bringing Optimus's face into view. The red eyes make the electronic approximation of Bumblebee's former leader look even more sinister.

"JOIN ME, BUMBLEBEE, AND RULE

BY MY SIDE WHEN MY DECEPTICONS
SQUASH YOUR PUNY AUTOBOTS."

"Stop this, whoever you are!" Bumblebee
yells back at the screen. "I know you're not
really Optimus. You're just a Decepticon
trick, and Team Bee's specialty is taking
you down!"

"TELL THAT TO SIDESWIPE…IF HE
RECOVERS!"

Bumblebee pulls back his fist and darts forward to destroy the console.

"Sir, stop!" Strongarm shouts, appearing in the doorway to the command center. "What are you doing?"

The Autobot leader turns around and takes in the concerned faces of Strongarm, Grimlock, Fixit, Rusty, and Denny, all cautiously keeping their distance from him.

"Can't you see?" Bumblebee asks, pointing behind him. "Somebot infected our systems with an evil version of Optimus!"

The teammates look at one another, worried, then frown at their leader.

Bee turns back to the console and sees that the screen displays a normal map, with only one bright red blip in the quarry. The flashing red eyes and clear outline of Optimus's profile are nowhere to be found.

"It...it was here just before you came in," Bumblebee tries to explain. "It was taunting me and threatening our team."

Fixit whispers to Denny and Russell, and the two humans leave the room, a concerned look cast on their faces.

"Bumblebee, perhaps you should let me tick...tock...take a look at your wiring," the Mini-Con says, rolling toward the confused yellow bot. "The negative effects of group management stress are not to be underestimated and can lead to—"

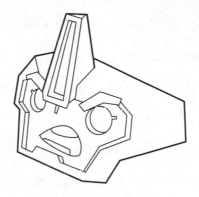

"Wait a minute," Bumblebee interrupts, taking a step back. "Do you all think I'm malfunctioning?"

Strongarm, Grimlock, and Fixit exchange glances.

Grimlock takes a careful step forward, his bulky arms outstretched.

"Let's all calm down, Bee," the Dinobot says, inching toward his leader. "We're all friend-bots here, right?"

Bumblebee shakes his head vigorously, clearing his thoughts.

"Grim, stop it, I'm not going to do anything crazy," he says.

The Dinobot continues to move closer until Strongarm elbows him to cut it out.

"I know what I'm saying sounds unusual, but hear me out. Somebot has been sending me evil visions of Optimus trying to distract me."

"I believe you, sir, but a tune-up never hurt anybot!" Fixit adds, approaching Bumblebee with forced cheerfulness.

"Fixit," Bumblebee says. "I don't have brain rust. I admit I'm shaken up by what happened to Sideswipe, but someone is messing with us and I intend to put an end to it!"

The other Autobots in the room look at one another with renewed confidence in their leader.

"But first we have a Decepticon that deserves some payback," Bumblebee says, pointing at the red blip on the screen. "And as Sideswipe would say, 'What goes around, comes around!'"

Chapter 9

Far away in the Realm of the Primes, a very disgruntled Liege Maximo stomps and kicks at the ground.

"These Autobots are NO FUN AT ALL!" he bellows, blowing up several fake bots.

"All I ask for in this vast, endless existence is some semblance of joy, and these boring bots are intent on keeping that away from me with their 'teamwork' and 'justice' and 'loyalty'! I can taste the fuel coming back up my intake valve!"

Liege Maximo's horns twitch, and a full legion of mindless bots appear before him, covered in all manner of slicing blades, blunt maces, and spiky armor.

"If all those awful Autobots want is some fight to destruction against a grand evil, then I'll give them the destruction they seek!"

"Who is Liege Maximo?" Optimus asks, his frame tensing.

"He's above your pay grade," Micronus explains. "Liege Maximo is one of us, an original Prime and member of the Thirteen. Long, long ago, Liege Maximo grew bored of our existence. He's never been truly evil, but his cruelty and penchant for manipulation are legendary. To relieve his boredom with the power he wields, Liege Maximo uses it to pit brother against brother for his own amusement."

"Brother against brother?" Optimus asks. "Micronus, before you arrived, I was attacked by something that took the shape of my teammate Bumblebee from Earth. It spoke in Bumblebee's voice and looked just like him, but the things he said…"

"That's Liege Maximo's doing, all right," Micronus says. "He is one of us, and we tolerate him, but his lies and treacheries have cost us dearly in the past. Now it looks like he's trying to have some twisted 'fun' with you."

Optimus narrows his optics and pounds his mighty metal fists together.

"If this is Liege Maximo's idea of fun, then it's time we twist it back at him," Optimus says with gusto.

Micronus laughs.

"Optimus, you're not ready for a Prime!" Micronus says. "You'll meet Liege Maximo in time, and he might even teach you a thing or two worth knowing down the line, but this is one problem you can't punch to scrap."

The Autobot leader's tactical brain races with ideas.

"The false Bumblebee's patience didn't last very long when I called it on its bluff," Optimus says. "It seems like Liege Maximo gets bored of his games as soon as they don't go his way. I think we can use that to our advantage."

Micronus smiles. Immensely powerful foe or not, this is one trial that his pupil seems ready to take on.

Back on Earth, Bumblebee leads Strongarm and Grimlock toward Skinkbomb's signal in the quarry. Fixit, Rusty, and Denny stayed back in the scrapyard to take care of Sideswipe. Bumblebee's and Strongarm's wheels tear rivets into the ground and Grimlock's pounding feet shake the trees around them.

"You know I have utmost faith in you, sir," Strongarm says to the yellow bot speeding ahead of her. "But even if you're not suffering from early symptoms of brain rust, we're still one Autobot short against a Decepticon that nearly turned us into spare parts last time we squared off against him."

"Fixit said Skinkbomb needs to consume large amounts of metal and flammable oils to regrow his tail-bomb. If we can catch up to him before he's eaten enough, we may have an upper hand."

Bumblebee shifts into a higher gear, spitting grass and dirt behind him as he goes.

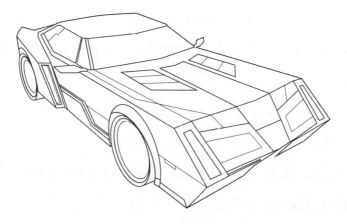

"And this time, I won't be so easily distracted."

Bumblebee, Strongarm, and Grimlock

arrive at the edge of the quarry in good time. The Autobot leader whispers into his wrist communicator.

"We're about to enter the quarry, Fixit. If you have any luck getting in touch with Drift, give him our coordinates."

The bots scan the rocky landscape for any sign of their explosive enemy.

They follow a loud crunching noise around a bend and spot Skinkbomb, chewing on a construction crane and guzzling barrels of oil!

"Autobots, it's time to ignite the dynamite!" Bumblebee yells.

This lame attempt at a catchphrase causes his teammates to roll their optics, but it does catch Skinkbomb's attention.

The three bots charge from their hiding spot.

Bumblebee and Strongarm, still in their vehicle modes, crash into Skinkbomb, knocking him off balance and causing him to spill the oil in his claws.

Grimlock leaps into the air and comes thundering down on the Decepticon, knocking the wind out of his pistons and pinning him to the ground.

"Why don't you try eating my Dino-Destructo Double Drop instead?" the towering Dinobot yells.

"You really think you goody two-treads could take me out that easy?" Skinkbomb asks, struggling under Grimlock's bulk. "Don't you know who I am?"

The Decepticon uses his pinned arm to tap at a button on his side.

A cascade of small spheres pour out of the containers around his waist—microbombs!

"Uh-oh," Grimlock says.

KABOOM-BOOM-BOOM!

A series of explosions ring out around Skinkbomb, the sound and vibrations echoing loudly through the quarry.

Grimlock is thrown backward, allowing

Skinkbomb to pull himself up and run back to the oil drums.

Through the haze of dust and smoke, Bumblebee sees that Skinkbomb's tail is nearly regrown. He has to reach the Decepticon before he can finish his meal!

The yellow Autobot leaps into his bot mode and pulls out his blaster.

Bumblebee lets loose a series of shots that opens up the oil container like swiss cheese.

"Looks like you've sprung a leak, lizard-bot!" Bumblebee cries.

His drink decimated, the aggravated Skinkbomb hurls the rapidly emptying drum at Bumblebee's head.

The Autobot leader ducks a nanocycle too late and catches the corner of the barrel. The force of the impact knocks him off his treads, and he lands facedown in a pool of spilled oil.

Bumblebee quickly scrambles to his feet, but not before catching his reflection in the oil—and watching it quickly turn into the sinister, grinning face of Optimus!

Chapter 10

Liege Maximo looks down into the portal to Earth, crowing in delight as he summons an evil Optimus vision to taunt Bumblebee during battle.

"Oh, is the little Autobot distracted by his big, bad friend?"

Micronus suddenly appears behind the fiendish trickster.

"Sticking your horns where they don't belong, Liege Maximo?"

The mischief-maker leaps up in shock, preparing to blast Micronus.

"Let's not bother with the knuckle dusting," Micronus says, hovering confidently in front of the horned bot. "We both know we're too evenly matched for it to amount to anything but a waste of time."

Liege Maximo's optics flare with anger.

"Time is all we have, Micronus! Don't you see how infinitely boring this realm has become? Manipulating these inconsequential Autobots is my new favorite pastime."

"Your 'fun' is done, trickster!"

Liege Maximo's horns twitch.

He makes a grand gesture with his hands and a smile cracks across his face.

"On the contrary, Micronus. My fun is NOT done....It has just begun!"

Back on Earth, Bumblebee pulls himself

up from the puddle of oil. Optimus's eerie face isn't a trick of the light—it's staring up at the Autobot leader with hatred in its optics.

"BUMBLEBEE," the voice echoes through the canyon. "YOU'RE A FOOL TO STAND AGAINST US. YOUR TEAM WILL FALL ONE BY ONE—JUST LIKE THE BOT YOU ALREADY FAILED."

Skinkbomb, Grimlock, and Strongarm

look around to see the source of the booming voice.

"Sir, why does that voice sound like Optimus?" Strongarm asks, drawing her blaster into a ready-to-fire position.

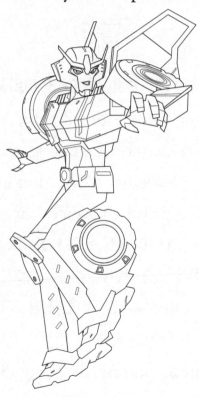

"Whoa," Grimlock says. "Maybe we've *all* got brain rust!"

"No, Grim, this is nothing more than a trick," Bumblebee says. "Is this your doing, Decepticon?"

Skinkbomb takes advantage of the confusion to scurry back to the oil drums.

"I'm not responsible for this spooky stereo act, but I sure enjoy dinner and a show!" The Decepticon begins shoveling metal scraps and great gulps of oil into his wide maw.

"You're going on a diet, Skinkbomb!" Bumblebee shouts. "Grimlock, clean his plate for him!"

Grimlock nods and transforms into his Tyrannosaurus rex mode. The brutish bot smashes his tail into the ground, creating a shockwave that sends the remaining oil cans rolling across the quarry floor. With another wide swing of his tail, Grimlock swats the metal out of Skinkbomb's claws.

"Strongarm, let's defuse this explosive situation!" Bee says.

The law-bot leaps onto Skinkbomb's back,

pinning the Decepticon's arms. Bumblebee dashes over and grabs hold of the nearly complete ticking time bomb of a tail.

"GIVE UP, BUMBLEBEE!" the imposter Optimus shouts. "WE DECEPTICONS ARE LEGION. YOU CANNOT DEFEAT US ALL!"

"I might not be able to defeat you all by myself," Bumblebee says, tugging on the tail bomb. "But luckily—I don't have to!"

Grimlock, back in bot mode, grabs hold alongside Bumblebee. With Strongarm keeping Skinkbomb's arms bound, Bumblebee and Grimlock succeed in pulling the criminal's incendiary tail loose!

"TOO LATE, AUTOBOT FOOLS!" the voice booms.

Bumblebee looks at the tail bomb in his hands. It's ticking!

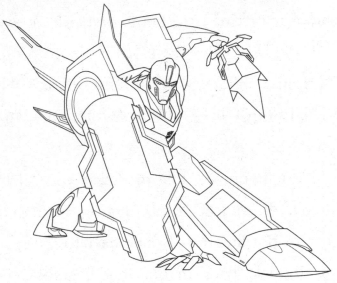

"Autobots, burn rubber!"

Bumblebee throws the bomb over his shoulder, and the three bots rush away with their captive in tow. They make it to the edge of the quarry before the force from the explosion knocks them flat.

KRAKA-BOOOOOM!

Bumblebee, Grimlock, and Strongarm stumble to their treads, their audio receptors still ringing.

Skinkbomb tries to scurry into the surrounding forest, but Grimlock quickly nabs the slippery lizardbot in an iron grip.

"It's going to take more than a cheap imitation of Optimus and a few firecrackers to defeat this team!" Bumblebee says proudly.

In the Realm of the Primes, Optimus

waits and meditates.

When his mentor, Micronus, left to confront Liege Maximo, he warned Optimus to prepare for an attack.

I have learned much during these simulated exercises, Optimus thinks to himself. *I may need more time and training before I'm prepared to face off against this impending evil, but I'm ready right now for any child's play that Liege Maximo can conjure up!*

A fog begins to roll across the ground, carrying with it ominous cries from all directions:

"Earth has fallen!"

"Bumblebee betrayed us all!"

"How could the Autobots abandon us like this?"

The red-and-blue Autobot leader climbs to his feet and calmly draws his sword. He speaks evenly into the void, no trace of emotion in his voice.

"Your tricks and taunts don't bother me, Liege Maximo. They never did."

Optimus's optics scan the fog.

Several figures appear in the distance, rapidly making their way toward his position. Malicious mockeries of Bumblebee, Strongarm, Grimlock, Sideswipe, and Fixit leap out of the fog and attack Optimus!

Optimus carves his blade in a wide arc, slashing through his attackers without hesitation.

WHOOSH!

Five of the six false Autobots fall to the ground and shatter into fragments of quickly disappearing light.

SKEESH!

Only the evil Bumblebee remains.

"Your confidence in these bots is misplaced, Optimus," Bumblebee says. "They will let you down. They are weak and easily manipulated!"

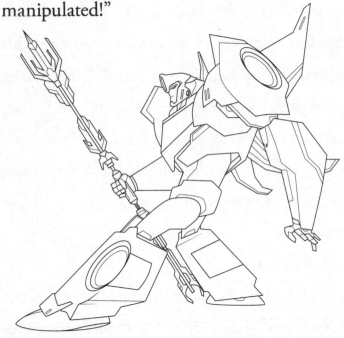

"I don't think so, Liege Maximo," Optimus replies. "Bumblebee and the other bots are the bravest, most trustworthy bots I know.

The only weak and easily manipulated one I see around here is *you*."

Before Bumblebee can respond, Optimus steps forward and drives his blade through the illusion, sending it scattering into flickers of light.

FWISSSS!

"Curses! It's not fair! It's not—" an angry voice echoes through the Realm before being abruptly cut off.

When Optimus turns around, Micronus is hovering before him once more.

"You done good, kid," Micronus says, a grin plastered to his face.

"Has Liege Maximo been defeated?" Optimus asks.

"It's not as simple as that. Liege Maximo

might be a menace, but he is one of us. The Primes will find a way to punish him, though. I promise you that."

"And his tricks?"

"Over for now," Micronus says. "And even if he tried again, you and Bumblebee are too wise for him."

"Bumblebee?" Optimus asks. "Did Liege

Maximo involve the real Bumblebee in all of this?"

"Oh yeah, I forgot to mention—that wily wreck of a Prime was tinkering with your pal on Earth in the same way. Confused him for a nanocycle or two, but Bumblebee shook it off just as quickly as you did. Seems he isn't too shabby of a leader himself."

Optimus beams with pride for his former lieutenant.

"You might want to give him a few words of encouragement, though," Micronus says. "Never hurts to hear a kind word from a friend."

He waves his hands and opens a portal to the scrapyard. Bumblebee and the other bots are gathered around Fixit's repair table.

131

Sideswipe picks himself up, clutching at his injured back with a grimace.

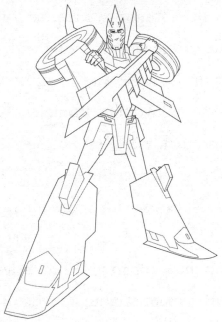

"Solus knows I could sure use a buff job!" he quips.

Team Bee feels a wash of relief that their friend and teammate is almost back to normal.

"Don't rush your repair phase, Sideswipe," Bumblebee says, gently pushing the younger bot back down to the table. "I think your heroism earned you a few cycles of rest mode."

"What would you do without me, Bee?" Sideswipe asks.

"Let's not answer that," Bumblebee says with a laugh.

With Skinkbomb safely deposited in a stasis pod and Sideswipe's prognosis looking better, the bots are looking forward to a little downtime.

Suddenly, their brief peace is interrupted by a much-too-familiar voice booming through the audio system.

"BUMBLEBEE!"

"Oh no, not this again!" Bumblebee says.

He pulls his blaster and aims it at the screen where Optimus's face has materialized.

"This is no trick, Bee," Optimus explains.

Bumblebee cautiously lowers his weapon.

"...Optimus?"

"I wish I could explain everything to you, but I can't. With time, I will. But what I can tell you is that you're a wise, worthy leader— and a fantastic friend."

"I knew it couldn't be you, Optimus," Bumblebee says. "There's no one I trust more on Earth, Cybertron, or wherever you are now."

The other bots look on with smiles as their leader reconnects with his mentor.

"I'm being tested in the Realm of the Primes, Bumblebee," Optimus states. "And I think you and I just passed an unexpected pair of trials. So, in a way, we were fighting side by side like the good old days. I'm grateful that Earth is under the watch of a confident, clear-headed Autobot like you, Bumblebee. You and your team have made me proud."

Bumblebee stands tall with his friends beaming around him.

As quickly as it appeared, the vision of Optimus begins to fade.

"And in some time soon," Optimus says, "I'll be proud to protect Earth alongside you once again!"